# Bordello of Vampire Pleasure

## Omnibus Edition

By

Lynda Belle

Shadowcat Publishing

San Jose, California

Format: Omnibus Edition

Author: Lynda Belle

Cover Design: Visual Effects

Editor: Claudette Cruz

Beta Readers: Alain Gomez and Lisa Frogjourney

ISBN: 0692730672
ISBN-13: 978-0692730676

To my husband
You're my pillar

# CONTENTS

Bordello of Vampire Pleasure 1

Bordello of Vampire Pleasure 2

Bordello of Vampire Pleasure 3

# Bordello of Vampire Pleasure

Vampire Pleasures Series #1

# Chapter 1

The blindfold felt tight around his head.

"We're almost there John. Trust us. You don't have that much longer to wait." John felt the gravel under the tire wheels. The speed of the car was much slower now. They must have turned off the highway onto a side road.

He felt his friend on one side give him a punch in the side. "This is going to be one night you'll never forget."

Laughter from his buddies drew his face into a smile. "I knew you guys were up to something when the dinner invitation turned out to be at a bar."

"You'll thank us later John." His buddy on the other side had the drunken slur they'd worked up to in the bar. "Really. I can't wait to see the look on his face."

The car stopped. He heard the doors open. His friend pushed him to slide out, but they still left the blindfold on, choosing to guide him by his arms. "Just let us walk you forward to where we're going buddy."

"I'm getting this blindfold off soon right?"

"Yes. Promise. OK, take a step up." He followed the instructions and felt the soft sensation of what must be a carpet. "We're going to walk for a bit, and then we'll take the blindfold off."

He let them guide him until he'd felt their pushes to sit. He rested his ass on a cushioned couch and leaned back. "So, is this it?"

"Wait. Just wait."

He heard his friend Jake laugh. "Wait for it. It will be worth it. We promise."

His other friend, Mike, said, "OK, we're going to direct your hands. Here you go." He felt one of them lift his arm and place it on something soft. He felt another hand hold his in place. It was smaller, and less rough. Hair touched the sides of his arm.

He heard his friends start a countdown. "One, two, three." The blindfold came off. He was leaning forward touching a woman in a red corset, her black hair brushing his arm.

She looked at him. "So, you like doing it with a vampire?"

He couldn't look her in the eye. "Where the hell am I?"

Jake shouted, "At the best vampire brothel outside of Las Vegas, buddy." Jake slapped him on the shoulder. "Happy Divorce! We're celebrating your newfound freedom tonight."

He leaned back from the woman, sitting upright on the couch. His eyes adjusted to the dim lighting. Velvety couches adorned the room, with other women walking about and talking to men in other sections. Large red drapes covered the windows, and all his friends were looking at him with ridiculous smiles.

"You can look at me, you know. I won't bite, unless you want me to." The woman spoke near him. He turned his head to see her swivel her hips side to side, adjusting her balance on her high heels. She licked her incisor points peeking over the tops of her red lips. Her breasts pressed against the red leather bodice. Her legs were donned in fishnets, and her black stilettos didn't make a sound on the red carpet. She leaned towards him, giving him an ample view of her peaks.

"Come on John. She likes you. This is the best cathouse outside of Las Vegas. The specialty is vampires." Jake's voice grated on him. He knew this had to be Jake's idea to break him out of his funk. His breakup with Christine had been ugly. Real ugly. She was taking him to the cleaners in so many ways. He couldn't walk straight with his head up anymore.

"And having sex with a vampire will do what?"

Jake answered, "This night will bring you back on your game."

He shook his head. "I can't wrap my head around the idea of having sex with a vampire."

"All you need is just a little taste of what she's got, John. And then if you don't like it, you could always leave." His group of friends broke up into laughter.

"Well, if you think taking me out is a joke?" John tried to hide the hurt in his voice. He knew his friends were trying to get his mind off the divorce. And the small slip of what vampires might be like in bed was coming back to haunt him. He had meant it as a joke really. He didn't think Jake would buy him a night at a vampire brothel.

Lucky for him, the undead had come out in the last ten years. They were accepted as an alternative lifestyle if not subhuman form of companion. Mortals were their friends now. But he still didn't totally trust them.

"Come on John. It's what we brought you here for. If you don't like her, we can get you another." The men were fanning out in the lounging area, viewing one vampire mistress after another. Their shirts were being opened by a few of the ladies. Other men in the room still wore the business suits from their conferences in Las Vegas. It seemed like a normal cathouse. He couldn't figure what the vampire appeal was.

"What is unusual about a vampire? There's nothing different that I can see with this cathouse from any other."

The woman vampire near him had been silent until then. "I can show you things no human would dare try. I can make you forget everything."

He looked over the woman–he corrected himself, *vampire*–that stood before him. She looked normal enough. Her black hair flowed around her face in gentle curves. Her porcelain skin was very smooth, begging for his touch, with her lips moistened to red perfection. She started to draw him in with her eyes. Her breasts pushed up against her leather bodice, accented by her fishnets, lace panties and high heels. She was gorgeous once he looked at her. Her gaze turned into a smile.

"Oh, he's gone now. There is no stopping him." Jack smacked him on the back. The alcohol made his slap harder than usual. John hardly felt it. He had gotten lost in the vampire's eyes.

He began to stand. The vampire woman eased out her hand and he took it. "Come with me, shy one. You are mine tonight."

# Chapter 2

He didn't know how he had gotten into the room. He remembered looking into the woman vampire's eyes, and next he was walking into a dark room filled with blue light, red velvet drapes, and black velour furniture. She guided him towards the bed, leading him to sit down.

"What is your pleasure, doubtful one?" she purred. Her voice held an accent that he was unable to place.

"Really. I think there's been a mistake. I'm not sure I want to do anything."

"We don't have to do anything. We can do nothing if you prefer, and just talk." She sat down next to him, leaning forward so her breasts looked dangerously ready to escape. She traced around the opening of his t-shirt along his collarbone. "You just keep distracting me with all this gorgeous flesh."

He tensed at her touch. She laughed, throwing her head back and revealing her sharp points. "You need not fear anything along the lines of death, dear one." She caressed his cheek with the back of her hand. "But you make it difficult not to be attracted to you. Who was it that made you feel such sorrow over love?"

"What? What do you mean?"

"I can practically taste the sadness that you reveal with your body as well as your scent. Someone is hurting you still. I assume it is a 'she' by the way you look at me."

She continued stroking through his hair, using her fingers to bring tingles to his scalp.

"She is my ex-wife." He stared at her. The way she was looking at him made her look caring. How could she be? She didn't know him. But he was feeling more relaxed the more she touched him.

"And she hurt you very much." Her caresses were going down the side of his face towards his neck. Her voice soothed his nerves.

He closed his eyes. "Yes. It still hurts. Finding her with my boss made it worse."

She tsked. "Strange way to leave a man. Heading straight to another." She stroked down his neck, circled it, and cradled his cheek. "I can be much more gentle."

Instinctively, he leaned towards her as if convinced by some inner drive. He felt her lips press against his. He kissed back keeping his eyes shut, trying to imagine Christine with him.

"No, not her. Whatever you think, I can make true. Be careful what you wish for."

There was a pause as she closed her eyes. He felt a tingling in his head, a weight on his mind. "You hold too much guilt about her. She is gone. I want to make you forget her."

He opened his eyes to see the smoldering hot creature before him. It was like he was in a porno. Her eyes had changed color, and her fangs were fully exposed. She looked at him with glowing red eyes. "I want to make you forget everything."

She moved towards him and he wrapped his arms around her, feeling the leather of her bodice beneath his fingers. Her lips caressed his. Sucking on the bottom one, she pulled it into her mouth and let her fang rest against it. The sensation as it pressed against his lip sent a shock through his core. Instead of frightening him, it awakened a fire long sealed.

"That's better. I want to make you less shy. We will take it all slow. Soon, you'll forget everything."

She embraced him, leaning him back on the bed. She kissed him until he couldn't imagine why he was here. All there was to his world now was this room. Just this vampire woman kissing him.

"Now John, I want to see what you are." She pulled him back up, freeing him of his t-shirt over his head. She smiled. "It is a shame to hide all of this." She traced his chest, feeling over the curves of his workout sessions and hard time in the gym to forget Christine. That name popped in his head only for a moment and the woman frowned. "A thought for you my love–there is no one but me now."

The image of the other woman faded, and all he could see was the woman before him, tight corset squeezing her breasts to burst from their leather keep. She licked her lips and reached to the front, unhooking the captives of flesh. Before him, her breasts slid out of their prison, nipples erect, flat stomach begging for him to touch. Or lick.

He leaned forward to taste her flesh when she grabbed his chin. "Not yet. You must wait until I say."

He obeyed like a dog, riveted by her words. A trance set upon him as he looked into her eyes again. "You are mine for the evening." She kissed him; her hands pushed him back on the bed. Her breasts caressed his stomach as she crawled up the length of his body. "You're mine. Remember."

She bit him. His neck felt the sting of her teeth. It froze his whole body. A fog took over his mind as their hearts became the echo of their union. He heard in his mind, "*Just a small taste my love. It will seal our connection for greater passion. It won't change you to a vampire. Have no fear. You have to drink my blood for that.*"

As the fog lifted, she hung above him, drops of blood smeared on her lips. He felt an invisible bond between them now. She was flush now with his blood. Her pale complexion had been replaced by a flush of living color to her skin.

He grabbed her by the waist. She leaned over the top of him, black hair falling around her. He sat up, kissing her, feeling the draw to her now that his blood was within her. A heat had risen in him that he'd not felt before. He wanted to take her. Beat himself into her over and over.

"That's it." Her intake of breath sparked his body. "Feel our passion." She kissed him, wrapping her lips in his, sucking and pulling them into her mouth. Her tongue explored his as they opened to let each other into the other. He lost himself in the kiss. Nothing could feel more passionate than the woman in his arms. Each pull at his mouth was an invitation to join her in something bigger than himself.

"Take me John. I am yours." Her whisper drove him into a frenzy. He pushed her back down on the bed, pinning her arms down.

"That's it. Ravish me." Her accent rolled off her tongue sending him into overdrive. Her naked torso had curves he wanted to explore. Taste. He licked down between her breasts, taking one in his mouth. He sucked as if he'd been thirsty for it his whole life. Cupping one and the other, he continued his exploration down her center, to her stomach. He brought his fingers down to enjoy the feel of her flat torso and round hips. His fingers felt and saw her body more than he'd ever explored a woman before. She leaned back to his touch.

"Take me John. I want you inside me."

A small growl escaped his lips. What was she doing to him? He found her garter belt release, and the clamps plinked the extensions to the side. He slid off each pair of stockings and threw them off the bed. He looked at the being before him. Eyes closed, black hair fanning around her. Her lips red and opened with the drawing of breath as she waited for his attentions. He took in the sight of her and forgot himself completely.

He slid her black lace panties down. He felt the lace, catching the smell of her sex. He tossed them over his shoulder. Reaching for her mound, he explored with his finger the place he wanted to thrust into. But he wanted to see what was the same between vampires and humans.

She was lusher than any other women before. His fingers flashed with shocks at the feeling of her body. Sizzling electricity shot through him the more he touched. It was drawing him to seize her. Her smell was intoxicating. The scent of fresh sex pulled into his lungs with each breath. It was the feeling of being drunk with lust. Thoughts of her only took over his mind.

He thrust his finger inside her, pushing and building her. He added more fingers to his exploration of her inner folds. He wanted to bring her to the peak so he could plunge into her wet opening. He saw her eyes open. "Take me John. Fuck me now."

He didn't need a second invitation. He pulled his finger out to tease her clit. Then, took his shaft, moving his hips to seek entrance to her. She moved back to welcome the plunge into her. He teased her at the opening, moving the head of his cock to make her react from the touch.

"Don't tease me anymore John. I want you to fuck me. Now."

He smiled. He'd never had more fun pleasuring anyone before this. Every inch of him took on a new feeling as he plunged into her wet opening reserved for him. The shock of entering her hit his system. More than any other time, the sensations escalated more than with a human woman. Euphoria took over his mind freeing him of all thought. He thrust inside her, feeling the walls of her inside recesses. He wanted this feeling over and over. She was like a new drug. "God you feel good."

"Yes. Pound me shy one. I like it over and over."

He thrust again and again into her, forgetting everything except the rhythm of their union. She responded to his movements, grabbing his ass to move him deeper inside her. He felt her hips angling to receive him more each time. Then the shudders started to take him over and he knew he was going to explode. "I'm coming baby."

"So am I."

The spasm of her muscles wrapped around his sheath, tightening around to make him release his load inside her. He collapsed on her, still buried deep. He kissed her and looked into her eyes. They'd returned to their normal hue.

"That was fantastic." He didn't have much energy to say more.

"We do have all night John. This is only the beginning." She moved and his shaft fell out as she took him in her arms. She bit into his neck so fast he didn't have time to wonder why she did.

The fog took over his mind, and he saw nothing but darkness.

## Chapter 3

He woke up in chains. He was in a dark room, naked, and chained to the wall behind him. His arms were elevated to the point he thought he'd lost all sensation in his hands. He squinted to get his eyes to adjust to the darkness. The musty smell told him that it wasn't the bedroom anymore, but some other dark place he'd never picture himself in.

It didn't take long from his revived state before she walked in. She was dressed all in black leather, her corset binding her breasts and legs sheathed in fishnets. The garter belt peeked below the bottom of her lace panties. She smiled, the fangs peeking from beneath her lips. "I see you're awake. Your mind is quite loud when you are."

"Where am I?"

"The second part of your package John. Your friends were quite generous with your care. They only wanted the best. I'm giving you the full works tonight."

"This is the full package?" He moved his arms forward only to have them catch against the chains. "How can this be what I wanted?"

She leaned down and cupped his chin. "Sometimes what we need isn't what we think we want."

She stood up, clicking her stilettos on the concrete floor. "Sometimes a more firm hand is needed to recover. I said you are mine tonight. And I am yours."

"How could you know what I want?"

She turned suddenly. "I've taken your blood. It tells me a lot. Can you honestly say you haven't thought of being taken this way? Held at bay by a beautiful woman? Tell me, are those pornos that are locked away in your closet all that you kept from your wife? Or the fact she couldn't put you into submission like this. After all, we've shared our desires. Now, let me bring out your hidden pleasures."

His cock started to harden at the idea of being taken against his will. She was right about the dominant and subordinate porn in his closet. It filled his hard drive on his laptop. He wanted her to take him, spank him, and do things he'd only imagined.

She smiled. She answered his next question before he phrased the words in his mind. "And you don't even have to tell me. I read your mind earlier. I already know what you want. And I'm going to give it to you."

She leaned down grabbing his face again. "Your deepest desire. Your deepest fantasy is my job. I'm here to serve you." She stood up and walked to the wall. There was a click. The light revealed a table in the middle of the room. "I'm here to give you what you deserve."

The light spilled from a single bulb set into the ceiling. The table was covered in velvet fabric, with a lounge device set into the top. It was a combination between a chair and table. He looked it over slowly then back at her. There were clamps at the end of the table, and chains by the lounge device. It looked interesting.

Before he could imagine what could happen next, she bent down and grabbed his face again. Her fingers caressed his stubble. "Do you trust me?"

"You're a vampire. Should I?"

He gave her a hard stare, and she dropped his chin. "If you do, I promise whatever you've imagined can come true." Standing before him, she straddled over his legs, her crotch waving back and forth in front of his mouth. "Anything you imagine can come true. You don't even have to tell me. Just think it. But," she bent down and grabbed his face. Her breath whispered at his lips. "You have to trust me."

He licked his lips. Staring in her eyes, he saw the hue change again. Her extended teeth poked her lips, and she swept her tongue around them. He built his courage to answer her. "If you can take me to places I've never experienced before, I'd be up for it. Especially if you can make me forget her. Forever."

She leaned closer, her lips caressing his. "You've got to fully agree. I can dominate your mind and you'll remember nothing. Do you trust me?"

He breathed in the taste of her mouth. Spices of wine wafted back to his nose. He took in a deep breath. "Yes. I'm yours."

"Good. My gorgeous one, you will not regret it."
She turned and walked back to the table. She
snapped her fingers and the walls opened.
Hidden doors revealed two other vampires,
dressed in burgundy and red corsets, silk
stockings and garter belts moved towards him.
He felt the shock to his core. The sight of them
coming towards him made him hard.

"These are my assistants. They are going to be
your wranglers."

The girls spoke no words as they walked to him.
Each was young, one with red hair and the other
a blonde. He was losing his self-control when
they undid his chains, helped him rise, and led
him to the table. His dominant vampire
produced a crop and slapped one in the butt.
"Faster, I want him bound quickly." She hit the
table and it made the other jump.

"Yes, Mistress" quickly replied the blonde.

They guided him to jump on the table, secured
both feet in the clamps and chained his arms to
the table on either side. He could lift his arms
slightly, but only just.

The two new arrivals started to caress his arms, feeling along his biceps and down the front of his chest. "No. I will direct where you can explore. Only at my direction can you play with him."

The blonde pouted and stopped. The redhead caressed one more time down John's right arm and the Mistress hit the table. "No. Only when I say so." The redhead exposed her fangs and hissed back for a moment. Then, she eased back from John.

John moved in his bonds, feeling the certainty that he was not going anywhere. The feel of the metal against his skin, rubbing and binding his body grew his cock harder. He was at the full submission of the vampires that surrounded him. He lay with his legs spread, cock upward and hard from the movements to get him in this position.

"What are you going to do with me?" It escaped his lips before he could stop the words.

"Patience, gorgeous one." The Mistress circled the table, waving the other two vampires back with her crop. She placed the crop on his chest. "I want to take you in. I want to inspect your wares, beautiful one."

She slapped his stomach with the crop, and moved it slowly on his chest, down to his cock, moving it to the side. The movements made him stir, moving his hips in response to the crop. "Good. You're sensitive. I like that in a captive. Girls."

They rushed forward, each taking up a side of John. "Only on my command."

They nodded. "Ursula, you are assigned to work his chest and neck. Clarice, you are the keeper of his cock." They moved to their stationed area, and smiled at each other.

"First, gently feed." She hit the table with her crop. "Now."

Each vampire bent to John. One bit his thigh. The other grabbed him by the neck. He didn't have much time to think. He was rushed into the euphoria of their feeding frenzy. Images of the woman kissing him at once flooded his mind as he arched to their rush of taking blood from him. His breathing paced their sucking of his blood. He was lost in the fog of their taking, his eyes closed with the orgasmic streaks flying through his body from their feeding. He heard the crack of her crop.

"Stop."

The two vampires raised their heads. John looked at them step away, and nod to the Mistress. Blood leaked from the bite on his leg. He felt blood escape down the side of his neck. The Mistress moved to him, took her finger to the escaped blood, and licked it from her finger. Then, she kissed him. He responded, enjoying the suction to his lips.

The Mistress stopped, moved back and motioned with her hands to each vampire. "Take up your positions again." They nodded and did so. John looked from one to the other, and down at his captive body. He moved his butt and his cock moved to one side. The blonde reached to grab it and the Mistress hit her with the crop. "Not unless I say so. You will be disciplined more if you disobey again."

She nodded and then looked at John. There was a hunger in her eyes. He fought his bonds again, wondering if this was such a good idea. He felt a wave of comfort envelope his mind. The Mistress spoke, "I won't let them hurt you, John. They may want to feed more, but I am their Mistress as much as yours. They will obey."

"I understand."

John's Mistress moved closer to him, her black hair falling onto his chest. "Remember, trusting me is all you need to do. Relax." She caressed his chest with the crop. The leather strap at the end created gooseflesh as it traveled down the front of his chest, down his stomach, around his cock, and down his right leg. "Leave your pleasure to me."

She pointed her crop at the redheaded Ursula. "Mount him."

The redheaded vampire got on top of him, sitting up on his legs, and grabbed his cock.

"Hold. You will not do anything until I tell you," the Mistress commanded.

The redhead nodded, and then smiled at John. Her fangs poked the tops of her bottom lip.

The Mistress pointed her crop at the blonde. "Build him so he is ready for mounting."

The blonde vampire nodded and leaned down, caressing John's jaw, and kissing him slowly. She caressed his chest and stroked his neck as she took his lips into her mouth. He felt the redhead moving on his legs, holding his cock at the ready. His mind was riveted by the attentions.

He looked at the gorgeous blonde creature ravishing him as she drew back. He smiled. "You are gorgeous."

"No speaking." The Dom smacked the table, and the blonde took his lips in hers again. He lost himself in the kiss until he heard the crack of the crop again.

"Prepare his cock." The crop sounded a crack. The redhead moved her hands up and down his shaft slowly, until a moan escaped John's lips. The blonde moved away from his lips and he watched her move to his cock. She grabbed the tip and moved her lips around the head. The sensations were the undoing of John's concentration. He watched the blonde and redhead vampire minister his cock, the sensations causing him to spill a few drops of precum.

"He's ready, Mistress." The redhead brought attention to his action.

The Mistress pointed her crop at his cock. "Lick him clean." The blonde moved her lips gently removing the drops of his pleasure.

Pointing the crop at the redhead, Mistress commanded, "Mount him."

The redhead didn't have to be told twice. She stood up on her knees and lowered herself onto his cock. The blonde directed it into the redhead's moist folds. John moaned as he entered her. "God, that feels, oh God, amazing."

"God may have nothing to do with this, John. But you can yell to him as much as you like." She looked at the redhead. "Take him to ecstasy."

She nodded and started to move up and down on John's shaft. Pumping him up and down, she rode him like a midnight cowgirl. Faster and faster she pumped him, while the blonde fingered his balls.

The crop hit the table. The Mistress yelled, "Faster."

They built him at the Mistress's command. "Faster, Faster." Crack.

He couldn't hold back for long. They brought him to the brink and he exploded. The redhead rode him back to earth. He opened his eyes, staring at the vampires that had brought him pleasure beyond his dreams. The redhead moved off him.

"That will be all." The Mistress pointed her crop to the concealed doors in the wall. They bowed to the Dom, turned, and walked to the door. One looked back. The blonde smiled at John. He winked. Then, they were gone.

"Now, gorgeous one, a break for your recovery." She moved to the wall, and pushed a button. Two more vampire women, both with brown wavy hair emerged. They wore black corsets, stockings with garters, and lace panties. It was seemingly the outfit of choice in the brothel. "See that he is restored for my ministrations later."

"As you will" they said in unison and moved to unchain John from the table. They helped him up, and guided him to another concealed door.

"Wait." John stopped and turned before the door in the wall. "What could possibly happen next?"

"You will see, gorgeous one. Vampires can cause men to have multiple orgasms. It's our specialty. You have a long night of pleasure ahead."

The assistants next to him giggled.

The Mistress caught his eyes. "You know nothing, John. I am going to teach you in the way of vampire pleasures. You may call me Mistress Shriandra." She smiled back, her points resting on her lips, making her into the fantasy come true.

The other two vampires grabbed him roughly and took him through the doorway.

# Bordello of Vampire Pleasure 2

Vampire Pleasures Series, Book 2

# Chapter 1

I drove with my foot to the floor out of Vegas. I'd never wanted to get out of a city so badly. I wanted to forget the last twenty-four hours, and the plan I had to do it would make my mother blush. I was going to go have some fabulous sex with a gorgeous vampire, even if it killed me. Just so I could forget the one thing in my life that had been really killing me. His name was Alex Lombard.

Alex is a rich playboy that I'd met at an art exhibition in New York. I was writing an article about different lifestyles of the playboy fabulous, and got a little too involved in research. One month of wining, dining, and incredible sex had led to him taking me in his plane to Vegas for what was supposed to be a weekend getaway. I found him in our hotel room with two strippers from the hotel casino. He tried to get me to join them.

I refused to and called him on where our relationship was going. I thought that the last month had meant something. He answered me by telling me to pack up my things. I had to get another room of my own and throw myself in the bed and take an Ambien to make myself sleep. Alex had flown off in his jet leaving me stranded. I felt used and abused. I had to find something to steady myself. This was more than just a fun fuck. This was a love resuscitation emergency.

That's how I found myself speeding out of Vegas, heading to the famous Vampire Pleasures ranch that my best friend Sharice had told me about. I can still remember her voice telling me on the phone how it was the best solution for my situation.

"There's only one thing to do for a breakup. Go fuck yourself silly at a ranch, honey. You're in the perfect place to forget Alex. Find one of those new vamps that everyone is raving about. Get involved in spoiling yourself for an evening. You'll never forget it."

I gripped the steering wheel harder, determined that this was the right direction. I glanced down at the map app on my phone, looking at how the arrow pointed straight ahead. I hadn't heard any directions shouted at me for a while.

I was starting to wonder if I was ever going to reach this ranch before I chickened out. No one knew I was going. I had nothing to lose. No deadlines to meet. A part of me needed to be scratched.

I wanted to use a man just like I felt used. Well, I wonder if you could call a vampire a man. Used-to-be man. The undead had worked so hard to be accepted into free society. A sort of coming out of the undead closet had happened fifteen years ago. But it was still hard to think of them the same as humans. They were something so different that the stigma of different still hadn't been removed yet.

I looked ahead to see the headlights illuminating the road. Nothing but darkness and a white dotted line lay in front of me. If I didn't get to an exit soon, I was going to lose my nerve. The dark silence was broken by the voice of Siri. "Turn right at the next exit in half a mile." I breathed a sigh to hear her familiar voice. It wasn't human. Just like what I was about to meet, but it was familiar. This plan was keeping me steady. I was sticking to it. If only I could find this vampire bordello.

"Turn right in 500 ft." I knew I was getting closer when the green sign showing the exit appeared. I exited, listening for the instructions on where to go next. "Turn right onto Pleasures Dr." I followed Siri's voice down a lone street, and saw lights in the distance. It had to be the ranch. As I drew closer, I could see what looked like one of those occult compounds. The buildings peeked above a high fence with only landscaped rocks surrounding the edge of the fence by the road.

I spied the gravel driveway with a gate open at the break of the fence. This had to be the entrance. I turned in as Siri said, "You have arrived at your destination." I pulled to the side where other cars were parked. Getting out, I looked towards the wide entrance of the ranch mansion.

It had a wide porch and looked built in the style of the southwest. A red tile roof graced the white, adobe walls of a Spanish-style ranch. Stairs with a red carpet up the center led up to the double wooden doors. Wide iron handles decorated the front of the doors along with carved panels of angels and devils. I approached slowly, looking at the décor. The lights were in sconces to look like torches. It all had a dark and mysterious feel. I smiled. It bespoke vampires trying to set the mood.

I reached to grab the door handle and was surprised to have it open by itself. Behind the door was a man. He grinned in a knowing way. "Welcome to the House of Vampire Pleasure, Natasha." How he knew my name, I wasn't sure.

I walked through the door feeling at ease in heels on the red carpet. I didn't have time to buy new ones. The kitten heels gave me confidence to look sexy. I walked further in and saw another man coming up to me with a tray of champagne. He leaned forward, and I couldn't resist but to take a glass. The bubbles glistened in the flute. I took a sip, enjoying the bubbles breaking against my lip.

I raised my glass to the waiter. "You know how to make a girl feel welcome."

"We are here to serve." He tilted his head downward and backed up to move down the hallway. I decided to follow him to see what would be ahead. Except I couldn't keep up. He whizzed away, and I found myself in a room that was like a lounge. People sat around in a dim light at tables and cushioned chairs. Couches lined the wall with lighting showing the people walking about. Women walked around in corsets, fishnets and garter belts. Breasts were ready to burst over the top of the lacy edges.

My eyes drifted to the men walking around with bare chests and tight black leather pants. Their pale complexions screamed in my mind vampire. I'd only seen them from afar. My curiosity was piqued. They looked like any human, just pale. Some of the men were beyond gorgeous. They were god-like.

One of the men came up to me and guided me to a nearby table. "What would you like to drink, beautiful?"

I looked him over. His toned chest and arms spelled model. He didn't look like a vampire until he smiled at me. His small fangs were exposed when he waited for my order. I broke my stare. "A glass of Zinfandel."

He nodded and dashed off. I looked around at the room. It seemed like it was set up like a nightclub, except there was a definite gothic BDSM vibe. The walls were black lit by more torch sconces. The tables had red satin covers and red velvet chairs were filled by groups of men and women. Vampires hung about them, enticing with drink or body language.

There was a group of men at another table boozing it up. They cheered as they clinked shot glasses and downed the contents. A booth in the corner was full of women. One of them had a bride's veil on and the rest were dressed to the hilt. Scanning about, there were mostly groups. I seemed to be the only one alone.

The waiter brought me my glass of wine, taking my credit card saying he'd keep my tab open for all services, and winked. I continued my people watching. As I looked about, I caught one man looking over at me. He was drop-dead gorgeous. In fact, he was the ultimate hottie. I caught his gaze, and he came over towards me.

Bare-chested and wearing the leather pants didn't do him justice. He was an Adonis. If he were carved into marble, it would make more sense. Nothing like him could exist in human form. But then, I was guessing he was a vampire. His light brown hair and blue eyes entranced me. He came over to slide next to me in my booth.

"You seem all alone over here."

"I am." I took a sip of my drink. I needed to steady myself.

"How could a woman like you be alone?"

"It's a long story."

"I'm ready to hear it."

"It involves a man. A man that couldn't keep his hands to himself."

"I do apologize for my gender." His voice had a purr of a foreign accent to it. I couldn't quite place where he was from.

"But you're not a man. You're a vampire."

He smiled at this, exposing his fangs. They were very small, but bespoke of what he was. "Yes. But there is a lot of man still within me. I am a man first. Vampire second. I can be your man tonight if you wish."

"I'm not sure yet. I'm just here looking."

"You wouldn't be looking if you didn't want to be with a man." He stared into my eyes. "There is a reason you chose to come here. To get away from the man that hurt you." He leaned closer. I could smell his musky scent. It drew me to him. I took another sip of wine. Licking my lips, I couldn't stop thinking what it would be like to kiss him. As if he knew what I was thinking, he eased in and brushed my lips with his.

"Helping you forget is my specialty."

"How do I know you're the right vampire for me?"

"We have a special ability to read a mortal's mind. I can tell you find me attractive." He nuzzled my face with his nose, brushing my cheeks with his breath. I could feel a connection, a pull to him. "If you let me, I'll help you live your wildest fantasies tonight."

I took another drink of wine feeling the buzzing effect already through me. "And you know what my fantasies are?"

He looked deep into my eyes. I was held by his stare. His blue eyes drew me towards him. Before I knew it, my lips were on his. He was pulling me close, his bare chest caressed by my hands. I was leaning on him cradled by his arms. I pulled back, surprised by myself. "What happened?"

"I helped release your inner demon. Something that humans like about us. We bring out the wild side."

"What comes next?"

"We can get a room. Or stay here. Whatever you like."

## Chapter 2

Before I knew it, I was walking back with him through a corridor balancing on my kitten heels from the wine. He held me around the waist. I had my arm wrapped around his bare chest. The scent of musk wafted from him as I looked over his neck and shoulders. I wanted to nibble around his whole torso.

What was happening to me? I never acted like this. It was like a new me was being brought forth by being near him. He stepped in front of a painted red door in a black-walled hall. He inserted a key, and we went in.

The room was the essence of a place to be with a vampire. Black walls and furniture decorated the room. There was dim lighting from fake gas light sconces on the walls. A red velvet bed spread lay across the wooden four-poster bed. A canopy of black lace wrapped the top and around the poles.

I had to giggle. I thought I'd given up my Goth years. But it brought back memories of wearing too much black in college.

"What's so funny?"

"It's how I'd want to decorate my dorm room back in college."

He turned to me, cradling my chin. "If you don't like it, I can take us to another room."

I brushed my fingertips along his bare chest. "It's perfect." My hands tingled, building a fire as I felt his torso. I explored his washboard stomach and caressed my way back up to his broad shoulders, feeling the hard muscles in his arms. I looked at him and noticed he was back to smiling.

"Now, what's so funny?"

"You amuse me. You're a vampire virgin. I like that."

"Is that all you like?"

"Your sensuous lips." He teased me by touching his lips against mine again. I couldn't take the touch without falling into him. I grabbed his lips in a suction I didn't know I possessed. I wanted to devour him. He grabbed my waist and pulled me closer. I lost all thought as I melted with his body. I released him only to breathe. I was partly panting. He was bringing out this animalistic need to pounce.

"Let's get these off, pretty one." He reached for my pullover jacket, and I let him pull off the sleeves. He placed it over one of the chairs, and came back to lead me by the hand to the bed. "Open your mind. I'll take you to your hidden fantasies."

"How could you? You barely know me."

"You underestimate the abilities of my kind. Remember, I can read your mind. Open up, and I'll do things before you even ask for them."

It was like he was enjoying himself. You can't beat the fact that he seemed to love his job. I didn't say a word as I thought of him ravishing me, throwing my clothes about the room, and taking me rough and hard. I was becoming unhinged by his presence. Animalistic was just starting to explain what I was feeling. I was starting to want more. I wanted full domination.

His face broke into a slow grin. "As you wish." He covered my face with kisses and leaned me back on the bed. Easing up my black dress, he reached under and pulled down on my undies. I felt them slide down, and then he yanked them down my legs and threw them.

"You can read my mind." He only laughed at my comment. He pulled me to sit up, grabbing the bottom of my dress and pulled it over my head. He threw it behind him. I heard it land on the ground with a *thunk*.

I sat up onto my knees. I was commando in my bra. It felt like I was free to join in the strip tease. I grabbed behind my back, and unhooked my bra. He watched as my breasts sprung forth and I heaved my bra as far as I could fling it. I heard it hit a wall behind me.

"I think I've unleashed a beast."

"A banshee at least."

"You're not one of those. But you are definitely an interesting human."

It was my turn to smirk at him. "What about your pants?"

I eased back on the bed, relishing in my naked pose. He backed up and stood, undoing the zipper to his pants. Slowly, he peeled them down his body, exposing a hard cock ready to plunge into my depths.

My heart sped up when I saw him in his full vampire splendor. His body drew my attention more so than any other person. His chest was porcelain, sculptured in the perfect human form. I hungered to trace over his curves and muscles. I wanted to melt within him. Be a part of him in more than just human. I wanted to be his. He was more than Adonis. He was Thor. His eyes glowed red, drawing me into his stare.

He came towards me. I felt the impulse to lean back on the bed, sinking into the multiple pillows of lush silk. I couldn't help but give into the relaxing feeling filling my mind. He crawled onto the bed over me. Easing his body down on me, I felt the feel of his silky, cool skin glide over my breasts and stomach.

"I must have a drink from you."

This stopped my wiggling under his body for a moment. "Will it hurt? You won't kill me?" For some reason, dying in his arms felt appealing. What was he doing to me?

"No. It is just a little drink. The drink will bond our connection. It will only feel as though you've been running a sprint. Nothing will become of you but feel closer to me."

I reeled as he got closer. The feeling of immediate danger stalked my mind. He interrupted my fear. "Do not be afraid, beautiful one. I will not kill you. I will only take what is needed. The feeling between us will be doubled." He began moving his lips over my lips, brushing the tips gently. "The fear you feel is the fact that I am a predator to you. The only thing that humans should fear. Your body may sense it."

He kissed me deeply, rising above me to position his sculptured body over me, brushing my breasts. His silky skin caressed me. "I am a being of choice. I do not want to hurt you. Therefore, I won't. I want you to live. I want to be with you this night. I'm giving you the choice. If you let me. It is up to you."

My mind didn't need much thought. His body was sending me into a spell of seduction. "Yes. Take your drink. Take what you need."

He was upon my neck before I could think much else. He pounced me and held me so firmly, fear erupted in my heart for a moment. Then, the feeling of euphoria kicked in. Pleasure erupted through my core as my life essence of blood drained into him. My mind grew foggy, and I could focus on nothing but our hearts beating together.

My mind dimmed, and I opened my eyes to see him looking at me. He kissed me, taking my lips into his with suction so perfect, feelings of ecstasy pulled up through my core. I shuddered as he pulled his lips away. "Don't stop."

"No. I won't. I want to take you to new levels of pleasure."

He eased down my body, feathering my breasts and stomach with kisses. Widening my thighs, he slid down and lowered his head to my wet opening. I let out a sigh, wondering what his lips would feel like upon my womanhood. He licked my clit, slowly drawing his tongue around my flowered entrance, and pushed his tongue in deeply.

I arched my back at the intimate entry. He lapped up my essence, circling my clit with his tongue, and clamped on with such suction it brought me to the edge with his first taste. I could feel my eyes rolling in my head as he built me to a climax, pushing on my g-spot in the right way. I shuttered with a full release.

The orgasm left me wanting more. He eased back up over my body, grabbing my breasts, pebbling my nibbles. I couldn't help but ask, "How old are you?"

"Old enough to know how to make a woman know the pleasures deeply beyond her imagination."

He kissed me, and I tasted myself on him. He eased down my neck, and lowered his body on me. I felt his hard cock circling for entrance, teasing me for a full thrust. I couldn't hold back. I hungered for him so much.

"Fuck me, damn it. Take me now."

He looked at me for a moment. Then he took his man's head, teasing my entry with his shaft. I couldn't hold my mind on anything but him. I wanted to shout his name, but realized I didn't know it.

It's like he sensed the confusion from my mind and answered my thought. "Call me Quinn."

"Fuck me, Quinn. Fuck me hard!"

He didn't need a second request. He kissed my neck as his shaft sought entrance into my wet cunt. I opened wide, welcoming the deep plunge I knew was to come. But he teased me. He didn't plunge completely in. He smiled and eased down on me, inserting just so slightly to tease. I threw back my head in frustration. I growled at him. "Fuck me now, damn it."

"Tell me how bad you want it?"

"I want you now."

"Hard?"

"Hardest you can fuck me!"

He pushed in again, this time just enough to drive me into a frenzy before he pulled back out.

"No, please, take me. Take me hard."

"How much do you want it, Natasha?"

"I want you deep in me."

"How deep?"

"Deep and hard. I can't take not having you in me much longer."

He eased back. Teasing my entry, his cock rubbing up against my swollen womanhood lips and then he slipped just inside the opening, kissing the entry with his cock's head.

"Quinn, put me out of my misery. Please. I beg you."

His sudden thrust was so hard my whole body moved back on the bed. I opened my legs wider to take him hoping for thrust after thrust. He didn't disappoint me. He pistoned back and forth, my thighs opening so wide to receive him. I felt God himself had sent him to fuck me this hard. Again and again he thrust until I felt my climax building to a release.

My moaning and panting built to spill out with a final scream as he thrust deep emptying his load within me. My yell of passion sent shudders of orgasm up through my being. Quinn collapsed on me, his heart pounding through my breasts. We lay in an embrace of our spent passion. I was feeling so alive, connected together with this strange being.

As I started to stir from our passionate connection, Quinn rolled onto me. "Do you trust me, Natasha?"

I wasn't sure why he was asking. But after what he'd just done to me, I was ready to let him do what he wanted. My mind floated in the haze he'd created from our lovemaking. I was his passionate slave. I couldn't resist him. I wanted him to do more. I longed for him to. "Yes, I trust you."

No sooner were the words spoken, he was upon my neck, sucking fiercely. My final thought was if I was to die, at least it was in his arms.

# Chapter 3

I awoke lying on a bed. The red velvet bedspread was underneath me. I was dressed in something that hugged my body. I sat and looked over what I wore. It was a black leather corset, similar to what I saw the other women wearing in the lounge. My legs had on fishnets, and garter belts attached to them for an overall sexy goddess look. My panties had been replaced with a thong. Damn. I was happy I had a Brazilian before my Vegas trip. It was to please Alex. Now, it was helping me feel sexy in this outfit.

In fact, I wondered how I'd gotten into it. Damn. These vampires were tricky bastards. Quinn had guessed right about me having a dominatrix fantasy. It was one I'd never really thought would come true. How was I to find someone that would be interested? He definitely could read my mind.

I went to roll off the bed, and found a riding crop lying beside me. I smiled. I was to play the full Dom roll. I tried to think of what Quinn would look like in his leather pants; myself instructing him on what to do to me. I smiled just as the door opened, and he walked in. Back in his leather pants, his smile glowing with his fangs just accentuating his full lips. "Are you ready to play some more?"

"Why am I dressed like this?"

"This is the fantasy part of your night. We specialize in putting you into roles you would normally not try in sex play. This seemed to be the one that interested you the most. I'm not surprised. You are a bit of a control freak." He crawled towards me on the bed. "I can tell from your beautiful mind."

"So, I can control you? You'll submit to me?"

"Yes. I am yours for the night. But I also have one more surprise for you."

He clapped his hands, and a panel in the wall moved back, and a blonde woman dressed in a similar corset and fishnets stepped through, leading a man by the arm followed by another woman.

He was stunning-looking with his light brown hair slightly falling in his eyes. His buffed chest had the slight brushing of hair up his torso, with a trail leading down to his larger package. I couldn't wait to see what he looked like bared before me. It gave me an idea.

"Strip him of his leather pants." The women, vampires I noticed by their fangs peeking over their lips, obeyed without question. They pushed him to lean against one of the bedposts. One blonde girl bent in front of him, unzipped his crotch, and wrapped her arms around his waist.

"Slow it down a bit. This is too nice a job to rush." I sat on the bed near him, and saw his eyes look towards me. He didn't seem to have any fangs, but maybe he just wasn't smiling to reveal them. He looked me over with hunger in his eyes.

The other redhead started to tug, pulling his leather pants to expose his tight butt. The blonde tugged down, and his cock hung as a hard mast in front of me. I had to smile. He seemed to be enjoying his rough treatment.

The girls finished the task of removing the pants, and held them, looking at me ready for the next instruction.

I stood, arms on my hips. "Undress Quinn as well." I looked at his beautiful, sculpted chest as he stood with his arms out, letting the girls unzip and pull his leathers off. He wasn't afraid to let his erection show. He stood with his arms folded, a Greek god at my disposal.

"Leave us." The girls turned, bowed, and went back through the panel wall door. I turned to the man leaning against the post. "Tell me your name."

"John." There wasn't any accent. Just a calm, strong voice with anticipation to the tone.

I smiled happy I'd watched all that BDSM porn on the Internet. It had filled my hard drive, teasing my fantasies. Quinn was right. It was my chance to finally try out some of what I'd seen. "Well John, I seem to be Dom tonight. I'd like to play with you for a bit. Will you submit?"

"Yes, Mistress."

"If there is anything you don't want done to you, what safe word do you want to use?"

John looked up at me. His legs were straddled as he leaned against the post. "Sapphire."

---

"Sapphire it is. You can call me Mistress Natasha."

"Yes, Mistress Natasha."

I stood up, taking the crop and tracing it down his body. He leaned back into it, posing using the pole to display his hot, naked body. "Damn, you are gorgeous John."

"I should say the same about you."

I hit the pole with the crop. "Only speak when allowed, John."

He nodded, and I smiled at the power of the fantasy. "Lay on the bed, John." As I watched him lay down, I looked over his steady erection, chiseled chest, and honed biceps as he placed his left arm behind his head. I turned to Quinn. "Your safe word Quinn?"

I heard Quinn answer behind me. "You need none with me. I will read your mind. In fact, you may need to use a safe word with me. Remember, there is always danger with a vampire. I will always ask you for permission to drink."

I turned to him and saw his fangs clearly as he smiled. The fact that he had to restrain from killing me was already getting me wet. The thought of dying in his arms still played in my mind. I thought it would be good to play with tonight.

I covered my fear with my next words. I had to remain strong and in control. "I want to explore both your bodies. Come here."

Quinn eased closer, but I put the crop up against him. "Let me move towards you. I don't want you moving at all. Pretend you're a statue."

Quinn stood as I caressed his torso. Feeling the smooth, silky skin of a vampire was something that was different. He was warmer than our first encounter. His musky scent had grown stronger, and it was bringing back the wild Natasha. I was going to have to restrain having him plunge into me too soon. In fact, I realized I had two cocks to play with. "What is a woman to do with two such gorgeous men?"

Quinn growled at me, and I grabbed him in a kiss. His suction was perfect as he pulled on my lips and pulled me closer to him. My leg moved up his body, wrapping around him. His spell was taking me in again. It was hard to pull away and take control. "On the bed next to John."

I went to crawl between them, and caressed both their chests at the same time. John sat up on his elbow. His torso was divine. His movements were solid and rugged. I looked at John then Quinn. "You will both compete in a contest. Each of you will be given an area to entice and seduce me. I will decide which of you does the best. The winner will win the reward to fuck me while the loser watches."

When I noticed both the men smiling and eyeing the other, I knew I'd hit a nerve. I liked being the prize in this game. "John, you will have my torso. Quinn, you have my lower half." I waited to make sure they nodded in understanding.

I looked them both in the eye first. "Take me, both of you. Now." I hit the crop against the post before tossing it to the floor.

John eased onto the bed next to me. I looked him in the eye, breathing deeply. He was so gorgeous. He grabbed my head, and took my lips in his. He was so soft and caring, pulling me close. I could feel his chest against mine stealing my breath with need.

His hands moved down my front, unlacing the bodice. I felt the easing of tension from the leather as it pulled open, and my breasts were free. John pulled the laces out of the holes, and let the bodice fall to the bed. He turned me towards the pillows. I backed up against the soft cushions. I fell back to let John take a breast in his mouth.

I stroked his angular face as he suckled one breast and then the other. Quinn moved to the other side of the bed. Leaning to the side of me, Quinn reached between my thighs, pulling the thong aside. I opened my thighs to him, letting him have easy access. I leaned back, letting John and Quinn take me to new levels of passion.

I felt one finger rub my clit, stroking the wetness at my opening, pulling and using it to lube my inner lips of my labia. My head bent back, letting the men take over my pleasure. I was losing myself in lust. I was beginning to let the Dom in me subside for the promise of orgasm. It was going to be hard to determine a winner. I could feel them both driving me into losing my mind.

It felt good to have so much attention to make me come. I opened myself to their administrations, relishing the passion they were building in me to release. Two fingers pushed into me, and I welcomed the entry by angling them to go deep. Lips sucked my clit hard. A tongue flicked at it next, taking me to new stages of mind-blowing passion. I felt suction on one breast with fingers rubbing my other nipple hard. My eyes rolled back into my head as I was set free to enjoy my slaves' work. I shuddered into orgasm from the touch of my sex slaves.

It took me a moment to recover from my orgasm, and then I was ready for more. God, it was good to be a woman. But I had to make a choice. I was still so fascinated by John. Was he a vampire? I wasn't sure. But if he was the winner, I could find out. I smiled as I made my announcement. "John, you are the winner. Your reward is to take me. Now."

John rolled on me, and I looked into his soulful eyes. Beautiful brown eyes looked back at me. He leaned down, kissing me. I pulled him closer. His weight fell upon me, and our bodies were in a desperate embrace to seal us as one living thing. I realized then he was human.

I was ready to play to the full edge of my fantasy. In fact, I was ready to burst through that edge and break it. I wanted it all. And I wanted it from John. For some reason, I felt drawn to him. Maybe it was because he was human. But wrapping my arms around his neck, I somehow felt whole. I had to have him for real.

I bit his top lip gently. "I want you to take me slowly. Drive me into a frenzy with your cock. But I know you're human. You might need protection, my delicious John."

He nipped my bottom lip back. "Of course. But I'm not sure where to find anything among vampires."

"Leave that to me." I heard Quinn's voice, and the sound of a drawer opening. I heard the sounds of a wrapper being handed to John.

He grabbed it as Quinn handed it to him. I grabbed it from John. "Let me. I am the Dom tonight. I make sure all of my men are fully prepared."

John eased back on his knees, and I pushed him back so he lay on the bed. Holding his erect cock, I ripped open the condom package with my teeth, threw the wrapper down on the floor and rolled the sheath over his full cock. I gave it a slap. "Now it's ready."

I leaned back with my arms over my head. John crawled back on top of me. "How do you want me to take you, Mistress?"

"Fast and powerful. I want Quinn to be sex slave to my breasts this time."

Quinn was so fast; I didn't see him move to the position next to me where he started kneading my breasts. He pinched a nipple, kneading the flesh of my breast to send sensations that shot through my core. John took his male head and teased my wet slit, gliding his shaft up and down between my swollen, wet lips.

The men got into a rhythm that was making me lose my mind. I couldn't help but moan from the sensations they were causing. John thrust into me, causing a shudder through my being. He thrust hard again, and I opened my thighs up to take him in deep. One slower, deep thrust and he started to hammer into me over and over. He jackhammered me, pounding me into the backboard of the bed. I came so hard; I lost the very sense of who and where I was.

When I came back to my senses, I saw the men looking at me as followers to a saint. John eased himself out of me, and stood up to remove the condom. He looked around for somewhere to dispose of it, and Quinn nodded to a corner. I heard the ding of it being thrown into the trash.

My hands were still up around my face, dazed from the pounding I'd taken. I felt so alive and full that I just didn't want to do anything but look at my two gorgeous men. "You both are amazing. You took me to a new height of pleasure."

John came up next to me on the bed. "You looked fucking fabulous coming like that. I don't think anything could have been more beautiful than you taking my cock so deep." He bent down and kissed me with a terrible burning passion. I had enough strength coming back to me to wrap my arms around his head and pull him back on me again.

"You know you two, I have one more fantasy in store for you both. I was hoping you'd enjoy each other's company. So, this next and last fantasy will be the ultimate finale of your night." Quinn stood, gesturing to the door behind him.

"What is it?" I tried to sit up to get a better look at the door.

Quinn smiled at me. "The only way to find out is to go through the door, and I'll show you."

I turned to look back up at John. "You up for it?"

"If it involves being with you, hell yes."

I kissed him back, and turned to Quinn. "Show us where we need to go."

# Bordello of Vampire Pleasure 3

Vampire Pleasures Series, Book 3

# Chapter 1

SHRIANDRA

I'd answered Quinn's plea to bring a human female with a lot of indifference. But when I saw him emerge with the female human, I was intrigued. What other human had he brought me to play with?

They led the way forward, the woman dressed in a dominatrix outfit, not truly the full style. I only let vampires wear the full outfit. Hers was a client's version so we'd recognize she was just playing. Not that I couldn't catch all the flitting, delightful thoughts flying from her mind. It was amusing. She would be fun to take under my wing for the rest of the night.

But John was my submissive and client for the evening. I needed to make sure he was completely satisfied. A quick brush with his mind exposed his thoughts filled with only the woman. He was in deep lust, responding to her dominant will. Interesting. Maybe Quinn was right. This had potential for some unusual sex play.

I came out of the shadows of the room so they could see me, letting the light fully show who I was instead of the shadows hiding me. The gasp from the woman showed my effect worked. John instantly went down to his knees, head bent down, and Quinn followed suit behind him, looking slightly up with a knowing look. The woman was the only one left standing, looking at me with a bit of confusion. I decided to put her out of her misery.

"I see you have brought me presents, New Mistress."

She smiled when she heard me address her. "Yes Mistress. I have brought these two to play with."

"Excellent. Sometimes it's more fun with more than one. Come, we have things to discuss." I took her by the hand and led her to a couch to sit. It was the usual client suite, with small table, couch, bed, and gothic decorations. I enjoyed the basics in every room. It helped to know what would be available.

Before I sat, I cracked my whip against the couch arm. "Come, John. I need you by my side." He got up immediately and rushed to kneel near my side. I immediately stroked his head, caressing his jaw line. He was too pretty a slave to not touch.

"He is yours then?" Her question sounded of disappointment.

"Yes. I thought loaning him out would teach him some lessons." I turned to her from my pet. "Did you enjoy him?"

"Yes. Very much so." She tapped her crop against the arm of the couch near her. "Come, slave."

Quinn was always superb at playing the slave. Sexy and pliable. He answered with a whispered vampiric voice, "Yes Mistress" that carried to my ears only as he sauntered to kneel by her side. Her hand stroked the front of his chest as he sat erect to be at the beck and call of her attentions. She relished the shape of his perfect torso. I admired her attention to her touch. I could even see the results as Quinn's erection betrayed his need to have her soon.

"Careful, dear. You don't want to lead him too quickly. Vampires are a sensitive bunch."

She had the decency to blush from my comment. "I do want to learn, Mistress." I smiled at her comment, letting her see I was a vampire. Her eyes grew wider as her thoughts flew through the idea that I was able to kill in one swoop. Then, she leaned back and raised up to face me away from her slave. "I believe I could learn a lot from you. What is the best thing to do with a slave such as this? Vampires are so different from humans. I know you must have the answer to my dilemma."

I laughed at this. She was charming. "Yes. Before I was a vampire, I did work as a lady of the night. It is how I became this, you see. One of my clients turned out to be a vampire. He rewarded me with this." I drew a line down my corset. "An eternity of pleasure for all now."

Her mind sputtered with the thought of giving pleasure her whole life. "Yes, New One. A whole eternity, never changing, giving pleasure to men such as these, with no changes to your body." I leaned closer to her, reaching out to her shoulder, stroking it and caressing down her waist. "An eternity to be with men like Quinn or John. Though of course, the human clients you'd only be able to see for their lifetime." I leaned even closer, brushing her lips with mine. The intake of her breath spurred me on. "It wouldn't take long to change you. One quick bite, and we could be together, forever as a team."

Her breathing had started to quicken; her breasts heaved up and down. I whispered, "You would love being taken by your lovers for eternity." I kissed her lips lightly, using the tips of my teeth to catch the bottom of her lip for her to feel their sharpness.

Her breath caught again as a voice said behind me, "No."

I sat up, turning to see John standing behind us. "We didn't come here to become vampires." His voice held a courageous strength.

I rose from the couch, facing him. "If you wish the game to end, you can use your safe word, John."

"I don't want the game to end, Shriandra. But I know she doesn't want to be a vampire."

"How do you know?" She'd stood up next to me, wrapping her arm around my waist. I pulled her closer to me.

Taking a bit of her hair in my other hand, I twisted it thoughtfully. "She would make a wonderful protégé."

Natasha interrupted me. "Maybe it's the future I was looking for. I could be the most powerful thing over men. Kill them in an instant." She turned to me holding my waist in turn. "The most precious gift of all. Free of pain for anyone."

"No Natasha." John's voice filled with emotion. "It's not worth it. Living is more than creating death for others." He grabbed her hand, pulling her close to him. "We can go on not needing this. It's not worth dying for whatever happened to you."

"How did you know something happened to me?"

"I'm guessing, of course. I had to forget someone. It helped coming here to do that. But now, I'd rather die than see something happen to you."

I watched the two stare into each other's eyes, lost in something more than what we could give him. This was working out better than expected.

I hit the edge of the couch with my whip to get their attention. "Then, we should have a contest. For Natasha's mortal soul. John, show her why she should remain human. I'm sure Quinn and I can convince her otherwise. Will you take on the challenge, slave?"

He pulled her closer to him, wrapping his arms around her middle, holding her tightly. "What challenge do you bid me to do?"

"Make her want you, John. Not as a slave, but for you. You have the rest of the night to convince her to not be a vampire. Quinn and I will try to convince her as well. We could use someone like her. Beautiful, charming, and hurt from the world of humans. She is a prime candidate to turn. She is going to be hard for us to turn down."

I turned to Quinn. Tapping him on the shoulder, he rose to join me at my side. I turned one last time. "You have one hour John. I hope you fail at your mission. Being a human is miserable business. You're going to have a tough fight." I slapped the whip against the couch arm again. "Slave, you are mine unless Mistress Natasha decides to become one of us. Come."
I strode through the opposite door, leaving the two humans to decide their fate. I'd won many battles like this before. I figured this would turn out the same as the others.

# Chapter 2

JOHN

I watched Shriandra lead the other vampire through the opposite door, leaving me finally alone with Natasha. When I was sure they were gone, I rushed to pull Natasha in my arms. "We've got to get out of here."

"I'm not so sure I want to leave."

"You're not actually considering becoming a vampire?"

"It's tempting, don't you agree?"

"No. I don't want to have to kill people the rest of my life."

"You don't have to kill people. Quinn was surviving off of drinks from me. I'm sure with a few clients a night, that's all he needs."

I pulled away slightly, but didn't let go. "You don't know that for sure."

"That's true." I moved closer again, caressing her hips and moving my arms around to her back. I wanted to save her, take her away. Something drew me to her, and I wanted to leave this place alive with her. I was drawn to her, wanting to kiss her, and take her on the bed. But I wanted her to need me to do it. I wanted to show her what it would mean to stay human. "Let me show you what it would mean to really make love. Not any sex games, but really, just me, showing you how I'm starting to feel towards you."

"You are feeling something for me?"

The surprise in her voice spurred me on. I closed my eyes and nuzzled her face as I whispered, "I've never wanted someone more than I do you. Don't let them kill you. You'll be nothing more than a slave yourself. Cursed forever into a whore."

She pushed me back. "That's what this is? Sleeping with nothing but a whore?"

"What do you think this place is? You wouldn't be in a palace. You'll be nothing but a vampiric hooker. Do you want to be that the rest of your life?" My voice went up in volume. I couldn't help it. "No, it wouldn't be for a lifetime. It would be for eternity." I pulled her close again caressing her face. "But make love with me. See what it would be like to be with a man that cares for you."

She rested her hands against my chest. "How can you just care for me now, John? What made you come here? Just some fun times?"

The taunt in her voice drew me back. "I was hurt. I think, just like you."

Her voice grew quiet. "By who?"

"My wife."

Her eyes grew wide. "How?"

"She slept with my boss."

She rested her head against me a moment, and I felt her sigh. It made me move my arms more around her and pull her close. "I'm sorry John. I didn't realize." I felt her cuddle up to me more. "You were right about being hurt."

---

"Who hurt you?" I answered gently.

She looked up at me. "I came here because my boyfriend wanted me to do a threesome."

"And you want more than that?"

"Yes."

"I can give you that." I pressed my lips against her, slowly at first, but then she kissed back, pulling at my bottom lip and slipping her tongue just slightly into my mouth. It was so perfect, subtle, and gentle.

"Show me what it means to stay human John." I was upon her so quickly, taking her lips in like they were my last meal. I knew in the back of my mind I had to show her a reason to live in the mortal world still. I needed her to want to stay with me. I suffocated her with my love, my need to show her that I wanted her. No one else should have her. The last thing I wanted her to end up was an immortal prostitute.

I whispered, "Stay with me Natasha. I need you to stay mortal for me." She kissed me back with a passion matching mine. Her arm moved up and down my back as I explored her thighs. My fire was a light in so many new ways. I couldn't let her go now.

I carried her in my arms to the bed across from the couch. The room was more of a hotel suite, and I was going to take full advantage of it. I laid her carefully below me, stroking her hair and head, looking at her. My Natasha.

This was so much more than before. I felt free to love her in ways I'd held back. Her breath was coming faster as I caressed her neck with my lips. She turned her head so I could reach in places around her ear and chin. Down her throat I nuzzled her skin, taking in the sweet tang of her body. I kissed the tops of her breasts, feeling with my fingers below the lace of her bodice.

I sat up to unlace her, spreading the sides of the bodice wider. She closed her eyes as I slipped a hand in to feel her full breasts. Squeezing one, I pushed the corset sides apart to lick the center of her breasts, kissing their full round curves, exploring the softness with my tongue.

Her legs moved, lifting in response. I felt my way down her belly, over the corsets edges to her lace panties. Lifting the edges, I kissed her breasts again as my fingers explored below the lacy sides. She was wet for me.

I lifted the lace and spread her wet lips to gain access to her clit. Her legs spread wider when she realized what I was aiming for. I moved down, licking her body, past her corset, spreading her thighs open, and moved the lace aside with my fingers.

I circled her wet opening before I plunged two fingers to finger-fuck her, using my thumb to rub her nub. Rubbing her in circular motions, I listened as her breathing turned to pants. Her moans made my cock harden. I could feel where I wanted to plunge deep within her.

I unhooked her garter belts, and they flung upward from the release, slapping her thigh. I grabbed the sides of her panties and pulled them loose down her legs. She helped, practically kicking me to help me free her.

Her legs moved in a frenzy. "Convince me to stay human John. I want you inside me."

I moved up to her, pulling my cock hard and ready to circle her wet lips. She moaned at the touch of my man's head, leaning back and whispering, "God, I love it when you tease."

I used my cock to explore her folds, feeling the sensation as her wetness lubricated me. I pushed slightly against her opening, giving false starts to help build her. "Please, John, take me. Give me a reason to live."

I plunged deep in her welcoming folds. The shock of entry sent shivers coursing through my body, propelling me to thrust hard into her. She moved against me, widening to take me fully in. Again, I thrust, and her moan answered my movement. "Harder, John. Fuck me hard."

I pistoned into her, over and over, losing count of how much except for the thought of her only. Natasha. Natasha. Natasha. Goddamn it, Natasha. Natasha. You've got to want me.

She moved with me, rocking in the rhythm as I made love to her, taking me so deep I build into a motion of no thought until she said, "John, will you always fuck me like this if I stay mortal?"

"Yes, God, yes, I will." Her pussy's muscles contracted around my cock and I lost my full load within her. My orgasm rocked me forward, and I lay on her breathing with her, and her heart beat with mine. I was dead to her. She had been the one to kill me.

---

I lay on top of her, feeling her caresses on my shoulders as I let the orgasm from our love pulse through me. I was hers. All I could think of was Natasha now.

I felt her soft kisses on my neck reviving me. "John." I kissed her back, and rolled off to take her in my arms. She nuzzled against me, fitting into my curves perfectly. I kissed her neck as I relished her hands holding mine, pulling them around her.

"What are you thinking, John?"

"That I want to be with you forever. Or die. If you become a vampire, you can kill me first."

She stiffened at my words. "I don't want to do that."

"Do you think that won't happen? I don't want to live without you now. Kill me and be done with it. Because if you go over, I don't want to live without you."

She rolled on top of me. "I want you to live John."

"Then choose to live for us both." I pulled her close to me, and she met my kiss. We lost ourselves in the kiss until I heard the door open, and felt her pulled off of me.

"What's going on?" I sat up to see Quinn holding Natasha by the hand.

Shriandra was right behind him, and eased to the bed, grabbing my hand. "Get up John. Time's up."

She grabbed me harshly, pulling with a strength I'd never felt from a woman. "Don't make me pull your arm out John. Come up off the bed. It's our turn to persuade her now."

I followed, knowing that if I didn't, no chance would come to save Natasha if I died before. I moved off, guided by Shriandra to the wall, in which she raised my arms and I heard a *click*. I felt cuffs around my wrists, and heard the *clunk* of chains against the wall as I pulled forward.

"That should keep you out of the way while we have our turn."

I pulled against the cuffs that she'd imprisoned me in. They held fast against the wall as I looked over to Natasha. Quinn had her facing him, caressing her face, to move into a kiss. I had to turn away. I couldn't watch his seduction. Knifes were assaulting my heart.

But when I heard movement in front of me, I opened my eyes. I saw Quinn leading Natasha back to the bed I'd made love to her in before. He was lowering her, staring with no words. She looked like she was in a trance. Her lips trembled and she took a moment to look at me. Our gazes locked. She mouthed my name.

"Natasha!" I pulled against my chains, leaning from the wall only to feel trapped, unable to stop her from being changed if she didn't want it in the end.

"Silence, slave." Shriandra came towards me, whip in hand. "Do not incur my wrath. It is only fair for us to have our chance to convince her." She produced a gag ball that she wrapped around my head and into my mouth. I was silenced. I couldn't watch the seduction of the woman I loved. It was the worst torture I had ever endured. I closed my eyes.

I was wondering if I would want to live through the night. For if Natasha chose to turn into a vampire, I knew I would volunteer as her first victim.

# Chapter 3

NATASHA

Quinn lowered me to the bed. My body responded to his as before. I was under his spell to submit. I couldn't look away from his gaze. I felt the fog enter my mind. I heard my name being shouted as if through a drum of water. I saw for a moment, John, against the wall with Shriandra. His arms hanging above him, pulling as if he was a prisoner. Shriandra nodded with her voice ringing in my head, "Enjoy Quinn, my New One. He will be the first of many."

I looked back to Quinn, his smile revealing the deadly points of his teeth. The look of them only begging me to receive them in a quick drink. He responded to my thought in an instant, nuzzling my neck with his lips. I leaned away so he could pull me to him.

I felt myself lifted, my head falling back as he began to drink deeply from me. My thoughts were lost then in the pulse between us, the passion that connected me to him. My very being couldn't pull away. I wanted him to take me, drain me. Make me his. I felt myself drifting into a void, away from this existence.

Then, the thought of John kissing me. Plunging into me as his body held me in rapture. It brought me back to my senses. I made my mouth move into words.

"Stop." It was the only safe word that Quinn would respond to. I was hoping his promise to read my mind would still work. The fog drew slowly from my mind.
I felt Quinn detach from my neck and pull away.

"I haven't decided yet." I turned and looked into his eyes. "You said you'd know in my mind if I needed to stop. You were right there." I looked at him and then to Shriandra. "Convince me without killing me. What would it be like to be a whore for my life? Then, I'll say, and only then, yes."

I heard Shriandra's voice answer. "It's not a whore. You would become a Goddess."

I heard the click of heels move towards me. "You would have men at your disposal. Turn them and they are yours." She came up behind Quinn, laying her hands down the front of his chest. "Any man that catches your fancy can be turned to be with you, if he agrees." She turned and kissed Quinn fully on the lips.

"You did that. To Quinn?" He nodded as I looked at him. I looked back at Shriandra. "For how long?"

"For three hundred years." She gestured around her. "This is my brothel, my dear. The men I've turned for my pleasure and the pleasure of others. But they agreed. They must agree. It is part of the New Vampire Order. No one can be turned these days unless they agree. That is why it is so important you choose to be with us."

Clarity dawned on me. "You mean, you really can't do anything unless I agree to be a vampire?"

Shriandra sighed. "Yes. You must agree, my darling. But Quinn is only the beginning. When you have found more men that you prefer, you may have them join you for eternity. It's amazing how many prefer it. After all, the alternative is oblivion."

I shook my head. "Tell me. If John and I want to leave, we can, right?"

Shriandra sighed. "If it is your wish. Of course."

I looked towards John. He was wearing a ball gag, pulling on his chains. His naked torso called to me. I knew if I left with him, there could be a life for me. If I stayed here, it would be for an eternal curse. I wanted more than that.

"I choose to leave. I'm sorry. But I want to leave with John tonight. Alive."

Quinn backed away from me, and I heard Shriandra sigh heavily. "As you wish, New One. It is after all, a choice you are allowed to make. I accept it. Quinn, free the other slave."

Quinn backed away from me, and moved towards John. He pulled out his ball gag and unshackled his wrists. John rubbed them as he walked towards me. "Ready to get out of here?"

"Sure."

He offered me his hand, and I took it. He guided me off the bed. "Where can we leave, please?"

"I'll have Quinn guide you to the exit. But I must say, I am disappointed. I will miss you as a new addition. Should you change your mind?"

"I won't"

"Very well." Shriandra stood up straight. "Escort them to the exit, Quinn. I think they are done for the evening."

He bowed, and turned towards a door. "If you would follow me."

It didn't take me but an instant to pull on John's hand and follow Quinn through that door. It was freedom from the hell we'd walked into. And bliss to leave it together.

I remember passing through a dark corridor towards a small room in which Quinn left us both. He nodded before saying "Safe travels to you both," and left us. There was nothing in the room but black settees and an open window that had "Checkout" above the top. I moved to see who might be there.

"Did you enjoy your night at the Bordello of Vampire Pleasure?" A woman sat behind the window counter, smiling, her small pointed teeth giving away her true nature.

"Yes. I guess so." I turned to John, grabbing his hand tighter. "I'm not leaving alone at least."

"Good to hear you enjoyed your stay. You are Natasha Carter, correct?"

I nodded my head to her question. Then she turned to John. "You're John Samson?"

He answered with a nod. She passed forward a printout of charges for drinks and basic services rendered. I looked them over, with just the basics ending just under a grand. But I wasn't worrying about the cost. I looked over at John, my newfound passion. In fact, I was amazed I was leaving alive.

"If you could both look over your charges, I'll check you both out." She smiled when she said this. I just looked at John. He shrugged his shoulders. I had to laugh. Who would expect it to end so civilized? I signed the paper. Turning to John, I gave him a kiss.

"What was that for?"

"I didn't expect to leave with anyone."

"Neither did I"

I kissed him. I couldn't resist. All I wanted to do was get back to Vegas and continue what we started.

"Let's get out of here." His voice was filled with the passion from earlier.

"Good idea."

We walked hand in hand through a back door to the parking lot, walking out to my rental car. I clicked the key fob to open the doors, and we slid into the bucket seats of the mustang. I had to turn to John. I had to know. "Did you mean everything? When we were in there? Would you rather have died?"

He leaned close to me, kissing me over the stick shift from the passenger seat. "Yes. Every word."

I smiled and kissed him back. I revved the engine, and turned the car to head to Las Vegas with a man I didn't plan on taking back with me. Stranger things had happened in my life, but this was the beginning of everything.

# About The Author

Just when you thought it was safe to go out at night, I arrive on the scene. Greetings darling. I'm **Lynda Belle**. I've always been with you, stalking you when you go to sleep at night. I'm part of your subconscious. I'm the naughty part that wants to come alive with fantasies that would make your mother blush.

I write erotic romances for women that want to forget reality and explore their secret, dirty love. I'm here to take you to those places. I've been hard at work writing new adult erotic stories to arouse you to new levels of erotic fantasy. Join me for some dirty love.

For more information on Lynda Belle:

Amazon Author's Page:
https://www.amazon.com/author/lyndabelle

Twitter: https://twitter.com/Lynda_Belle

Website/Blog: http://lyndabelle.com

Newsletter: http://eepul.com/bdhOr5

## Acknowledgments

I'd like to thank all of the erotica writers on Kboards.com. Your tips have been invaluable. Lisa and Alain, thanks for being able to take on this project at the last minute. You totally Queen Latifah'ed it. Claudette, thanks for the editing eye you turn onto my manuscripts. You know how to crack all my projects into shape. And to all of you, my readers. You keep me going to pound out story after story. This is all for you.

If you enjoyed this book, please feel free to express your opinion in a review on Amazon or Goodreads. I would appreciate the feedback. –Lynda Belle

**Other hot erotic tales by Lynda Belle:**

**Scottish Erotic Tales:**

Highlander Bride Taken
Highlander Bride Seduction
Highlander Bride Freedom

**Hot Groupies Series:**

Rockin' Him Hard
Rockin' Him Harder
Rockin' Him Fierce

On Call Series:

The Perfect Escort:
The Perfect Date

Exhibitionists Encounters Series

The Day I Met Her
The Night I Met Him

***All ebooks are Kindle Unlimited titles.

**Soon to be available as omnibus print editions.